A Bird in Paris

by

KAY FENDER

illustrations by

PHILIPPE DUMAS

PRENTICE-HALL, INC.

ENGLEWOOD CLIFFS, NEW JERSEY

Printed in Great Britain
Prentice-Hall, Inc., Englewood Cliffs, New Jersey
Prentice-Hall of Canada, Scarborough, Ontario, Canada

Library of Congress Cataloging in Publication Data
Fender, Kay. Odette: a bird in Paris.
SUMMARY: An old man who plays an accordion in the subway befriends a
young bird. (1. Birds--Fiction. 2. Paris--Fiction)
i. Dumas, Philippe. ii. Title.
PZ7.F33770d3   (E)   77-6352
ISBN 0-13-630525-3

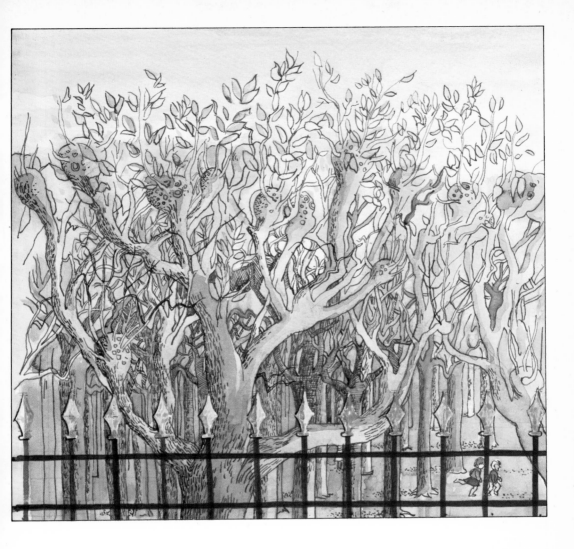

Not so very long ago, when spring came to Paris,
each branch of every tree in the park was bright
with tiny green leaves. One old tree was so big it
towered over the other trees, stretched over the
fence to the street outside, and down to the steps of
the Metro station.

Two young birds chose this tree for their home. In its topmost branches, they built their first nest, just the right size for two birds. Here they laid their eggs, and sat on them until they hatched. As the eggs cracked open, the baby birds filled the nest.

When the last bird hatched,
there was no room left in the
nest and the youngest bird
fell down,
    down,
    down

and landed on the hard straw hat of an old man, who was on his way down the steps of the Metro.

The baby bird was frightened. She held on to the hat
with all her might

as the old man came to the bottom of the steps and walked into a long, bright tunnel.

Setting his stool against the wall of the tunnel, the old man sat down and began to play his accordion. The bird stayed very still. The music made her feel safe and happy.

At last, she decided to ask this nice old man for help.
She hopped to the edge of the hat, and peered over
it. "Poor little bird," the old man said. "You must have
fallen out of your nest. I will put you back."

He looked up, but down in the Paris Metro there
were no birds' nests anywhere.

"I wonder where you came from," the old man said
to the baby bird.

He took her in his hand. "I'll just have to take you
home and look after you myself," he said.

The old man went to sleep worrying about the baby
bird, but when he woke up the next morning the
bird was sleeping peacefully on top of his straw hat.

"Now I must give her a name. Odette? Yes, I will call her Odette." And he fed her a breakfast of warm milk through an eye dropper.

"Now, Odette," the old man said, "it is time for me to
go to work."
The little bird went with him happily.

So they walked together through the city to the
Metro. The little bird didn't miss her mother and
father any more. The old man wasn't lonely either,
and he walked straight and tall.

Odette helped the old man make music.

People began to notice a smile on the old man's face
for the first time.

Day after day, the old man and the little bird played
beautiful music in the Metro.

Wherever the old man went, Odette went too.

They even shared lunch together.

Every Sunday, the two of them went to the park to
watch the children play.

It was summertime, and Odette loved to fly high
into the trees, so high the old man could no longer
see her, even though she could see him.

When autumn came, the leaves on the trees turned
yellow and the birds Odette met in the park began
to talk of flying south for the winter. They asked
Odette to come with them.

She told the old man, and asked him what she should do.

"It will be too cold for you here, Odette," the old man answered. "If your friends and your cousins and brothers and sisters are all flying south to be in the sun, I think you should go too."

So Odette left with the other birds one cold, bright day, and the old man could not find Odette in the crowd to wave goodbye to her.

He still played his accordion in the Metro, but his smile disappeared. There was no one to tease him, and to cheer him up. The winter wind blew cold.

One night the old man wrote Odette a letter, telling her how much he missed her. He went to mail it, but he remembered then that he had not taught Odette how to read yet. He sighed and walked home in the cold rain.

Spring came, and Odette started north. She was in a
hurry to see the old man, and to introduce him to
her new mate. She flew straight to the Metro
station, but the old man was not there.

They circled over the steps, and there, high in the
branches of a tree was the old man's hat.

Odette knew then that the old man would never
again play his accordion in the Metro. She was very
sad.

Today Odette lives in the hard straw hat the old man left her. She laid her eggs there, and now she teaches her babies the songs the old man used to play on his accordion.